I JUST LIKE YOU

Suzanne Bloom

BOYDS MILLS PRESS
An Imprint of Highlights
Honesdale, Pennsylvania

Boyds Mills Press
An Imprint of Highlights
815 Church Street
Honesdale, Pennsylvania 18431
boydsmillspress.com
Printed in China

ISBN: 978-1-62979-878-3
Library of Congress Control Number: 2017949847

First edition
The text of this book is set in Hoosker Dont.
The illustrations are done in pencil and watercolor.

10 9 8 7 6 5 4 3 2 1

To our two new daughters,
Harmony & Laura,
daring, determined, and delightfully different

You don't look
just like me.

You don't
see the
things I see.

You don't walk
just like me.

You don't talk
just like me.

You just **like** me!

You just **like** me!

You just **like** me!

I like
your flip-flops.

Thank
you.

I like
your glasses.

You do?

I like
to build things.
Do you?

I like to
take my time.

I'm
speedy.

You are tall.

Yes, indeedy.

Let's be
dancy.

Let's be
fancy.

Sometimes
I'm shy.

So am I.

So am I.

You like
exploring.

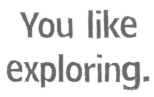

I do too.

I like stories,
just like you.

So, even though
I don't dress
just like you,

or do my hair
like you do.

I don't eat
just like you,

or even read
just like you.

I just
like you!

I just
like you!

I just **like** you!
Yes, I do.